The Jazz of Our Street

BY *Fatima Shaik*   PICTURES BY *E.B. Lewis*

Dial Books for Young Readers  New York

Special thanks to Ellis Marsalis for checking the facts in this book.

Published by Dial Books for Young Readers
A member of Penguin Putnam Inc.
375 Hudson Street
New York, New York 10014

Typography by Amelia Lau Carling
Printed in Hong Kong
First Edition
1 3 5 7 9 10 8 6 4 2

Library of Congress Cataloging in Publication Data
Shaik, Fatima, date.
The jazz of our street/by Fatima Shaik; pictures by E. B. Lewis. 1st ed.
p. cm.
Summary: Two siblings dash from their porch one morning
to join the second-line parade stamping, swaying, and dancing
behind the jazz band marching through their
New Orleans neighborhood.
ISBN 0-8037-1885-3 (trade). ISBN 0-8037-1886-1 (lib. bdg.)
[1. Jazz—Fiction. 2. New Orleans (La.)—Fiction. 3. Afro-Americans—Fiction.]
I. Lewis, Earl B., ill. II. Title.
PZ7.S52785Jaz 1998 [E]—dc21 97-12377 CIP AC

The full-color artwork was prepared using watercolors. The painting on page 19
is based on a photograph © 1964, 1997 by Maurice M. Martinez.

To Celeste and Sophia with love and music—F. S.

To the members of the ReBirth Brass Band
with heartfelt thanks for all their help—E. B. L.

The big drum's sounds
say, "Come! Come! Come!"
So Brother and I run from our porch
to the wide morning street.

There we greet our neighbors—
old folks and teenagers,
and fathers and mothers
who dropped their pounding hammers
and stopped cleaning mid-sweep—

to meet the jazz band that calls us with its beat.

The drum's rhythms tell us
we will have a parade
even though it's not a holiday.

In New Orleans, and especially
here in our neighborhood of Tremé,
we have music the way other folks talk.

So where some people might gather for speeches
to remember the dead,
honor births and great days in history,

or just celebrate as we do today—

we follow a band
to listen and dance
in our own special way.

Here are the instruments
ready to play.
The tuba, trombone, and trumpet
we nickname "the big mouths."
The saxophone makes
a squeak.

The band warms up
with odd, jumping notes
that don't seem to match.
But then they mend into harmony.

The band members wear serious looks on their faces,
like travelers from many distant parts of the world
who understand only the language of sound.

Each listens real hard
when another has something to say,
because all must play along—
not just with the songs.

Each must help
the others weave
their own musical stories
into the sounds of today's parade.

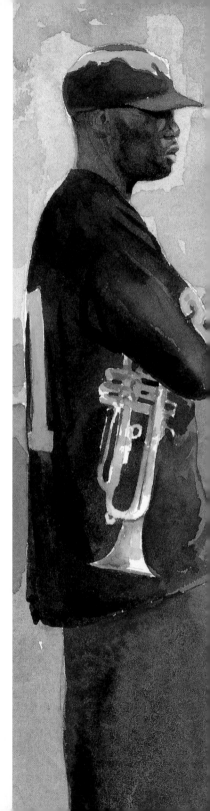

Just like the voices Brother and I hear
in the gathering crowd:
"How you, baby?"
"Where your mama and them?"

Each person blends
into our choir of greetings
in her own way.

But then the drum talks.
The reed squawks.
The trombone honks.

And everyone halts
at the sound of the first song beginning.
Brother and I join the crowd
to shout in answer, "Hey!"

The band begins with a smooth sound
like a baby's coo to a breeze
that finds its way through the sizzling heat.

Then the horns rise to a chuckle,
like the laughter of cooks
who stand behind screen windows
cracking crab shells for crabmeat.

Then the music sways like grandmothers walk—
silence, then heavy breath.
The sound is like slippers slapping and scraping
on the long gravel streets.

The songs growl like mad boys who fall
too hard to their beds.

Then they rumble and hum like men
who carry home at daybreak tunes
full of memories of
hard work and good times.

And when these feelings push out
through all the instruments at once,
"It's a jazz," the people around say.

All Brother and I know
as we stand in the street
is this beat
has the rising and falling of
lifting and calling,
stamping and hauling
we hear on our block every day.

Then the band rings out
a note that tells us
soon we will begin rambling.
It is our style of moving to the music.
It can be funny and lively, or
reverent and sad.

We gather in one second
behind the band,
and we wait for the next part of our ceremony—
the music's command.

Then all instruments, bodies, and breath
break open in one cheer,
"Yeah!"

The dancing begins!

In the crowd, hands reach to heaven
and fingers snap.
Through the air, elbows swim.

Hips shake to the pavement,
shoulders shimmy up with the melody
like fish leaping from rivers.
To the beat of the drums, backbones slink.

The feeling is like ice water
raining in one-hundred-degree heat.

The sound is like being lifted off earth
and being carried far, far away.

We sing in our minds
"Down by the Riverside,"
while our feet join in the parade.

Feeling our own shining and joy in being alive,
we walk with the happy spirits of the dead

like Louis Armstrong, our musician,
Marie Laveau, hairdresser and politician,
and the writers Desdunes, Dalcour, and Lanusse.

We think of so many Tremé people,
both famous and not,
when we pass the old cemetery gates.

We follow their paths as we dance and walk.
We shimmy. We shake like a rumbling train,
remembering the times before.

Past the gingerbread houses,
over mud and brick sidewalks our neighbors laid,
we slip down, jump around, laugh, and holler, "No more!"

We bounce off the ground
in our dance of the street.
Then the bass drum reminds us,
"Peace! Peace! Peace!"

Now the music stops and we pause in one breath
to silently recollect the reason
we gather together at all:

Because the tradition
of love is our mission.

We remember how proud people came here
from far away and long ago,
and now their children, and their children live
in our neighborhood homes.

We remember through the instruments' talk
the language of dance,
and the feeling in our hearts.

We remember when we form into a last circle
at the end of our long walk.

This ceremony of dancing
to the beat of our emotions
is called the second line.

We have passed it down in New Orleans
from parent to child, and neighbor to friend
for a very long time.

And the spirit of memories we create
moves like a volcano up and down the street.
Music spills out in dancing through all the people
who are caught by the second-line beat.

Some jump up.
Some go low and rock their hips to the pavement.
Some lie down dancing in the dust.

And Brother and I feel the solid earth
and the peace of heaven too
are inside of us.

We see the old people smile
and the children skip
and the folk gone and forgotten
called and remembered again.

The last, loose notes of the band
are as ancient and familiar
as the nearby babbling river,
and they sound sweet as our own names.

Then we go back to our porches.
The morning is over,
but Brother and I are feeling just fine.

Because the band called us today,
and we pranced, played, and swayed
in the time-honored way
in New Orleans, where music found feet.
We marched in Tremé
to the jazz of our street.

Author's Note

The roots of jazz music are in the jazz marching bands that originated in New Orleans before the turn of the 20th century. The marching bands were hired for many occasions—church fairs, funerals, small business openings, and parties—because of their popularity with local audiences. And following the bands as they wound through neighborhoods, a "second line" of people would dance.

The bands played spirituals or local standards such as "Down by the Riverside" with staggered rhythms to make the music "jazzy." These syncopated rhythms were echoed in the dance movements of the second liners, who would move up and down and sway shoulders, hips, and back in time to the beat in a "call and response" pattern. Many of the dance movements have been traced to West Africa, and the call and response pattern is itself an African musical tradition.

The second-line dances have been passed down through generations largely by observation and repetition in informal settings. However, the socials, funerals, and parades of the city's benevolent organizations gave formal occasions for the teaching of the history and movements of the dance. The oldest of these still in existence is "The Young Men Olympians," incorporated in 1885.

Since the 1970's there has been a resurgent interest in second lining with the formation of new organizations in Tremé such as "Tambourine and Fan," "Money Wasters," "Calendar Girls," "The Young and True Friends," "Scene Boosters," and "The Jolly Bunch."